BAKE SALE
Sara Varon

:01
First Second
New York & London

:01

First Second
New York & London

Published by First Second
First Second is an imprint of Roaring Brook Press,
a division of Holtzbrinck Publishing Holdings Limited Partnership
175 Fifth Avenue, New York, New York 10010

Distributed in the United Kingdom by Macmillan Children's Books,
a division of Pan Macmillan.

Book design by Sara Varon & Colleen AF Venable

Cataloging-in-Publication Data is on file with the Library of Congress

Paperback ISBN 978-1-59643-419-6
Hardcover ISBN 978-1-59643-740-1

First Second books are available for special promotions and premiums.
For details, contact: Director of Special Markets, Holtzbrinck Publishers.

FIRST
EDITION

First edition 2011
Printed in March 2011 in China
by South China Printing Co. Ltd., Dongguan City, Guangdong Province

Paperback: 10 9 8 7 6 5 4 3 2 1
Hardcover: 10 9 8 7 6 5 4 3 2 1

BY ART
WE LIVE

chapter

one

(Flour mixture)

(muffin tin)

7:45 A M

(convection oven!)

turbofan

(Frosting)

(spatula)

8:30 A M

7

Oh, Cupcake, it looks delicious.

(marzipan carrot)

My gardening club goes crazy for your carrot cake.

Are you ready for band practice? The 4th of July parade is right around the corner.

Let's stop by the coffee shop on the way and get something to eat . . . I'm starving.

Yeah, she's a big celebrity now, but we go way back. She's been my aunt's business partner since I was a little eggplant on the vine. She's the pastry chef and candy-maker at their restaurant.

Wow!

You know Turkish Delight?! I can't believe you never told me— she's my idol!

Yeah, she's pretty cool. Come on. We're going to be late for band practice. I'll pay if you get the tip.

23

the following week...

press!

347-9571

ring! ring!

Hi, Cupcake! I'm thinking about going to the Turkish Baths this afternoon in honor of my upcoming trip.

Will you come with me?

Sure! See You at 4?

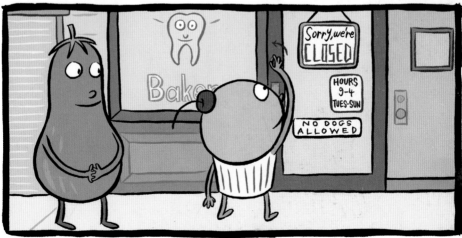

Sorry, we're CLOSED

HOURS 9-4 TUES-SUN

NO DOGS ALLOWED

heater

I don't think this dry heat is good for my frosting... Let's try the Turkish Room?

Sounds good to me.

44

47

52

press!

Hi, Eggplant! I was thinking about what you said... Do you think the band would mind if I took a break for a while?

I bet they would understand. Besides, I think Avocado wanted to try his hand at the drums.

PAINT

Avocado?! Well, I guess that would be okay... I already have some ideas about how I can make extra money.

Well, if you ever need someone to work at the bakery on the weekend, I can be your cashier.

Would you really?! Thanks, Eggplant! You are the best friend a baked good could wish for!

HOW TO MAKE
SUGARED FLOWERS

ingredients

1. One dozen freshly cut, pesticide-free, edible flowers
2. 4 teaspoons meringue powder
3. One cup superfine sugar
4. water

you will also need:

scissors, tweezers, small bowl, container for mixing meringue powder, wax paper, watercolor paint-brush, and a tray or cookie sheet for drying your flowers

Some common edible flowers:
(NOTE: Be sure they are pesticide-free)

Daisies

Nasturtiums

Lavender

Marigolds

Roses

Pansies

Violets

1. Pull petals from flowers. The white bases of the petals (especially on roses) may be bitter, so trim them off.

2. Rinse flowers to remove dirt and check for insects. To rinse, fill small bowl with lightly salted cool water and dip each petal. Afterwards, quickly dip petals in very cold water to perk them up. Air dry on paper towel. Petals must be completely dry before proceeding.

3. In a small bowl, dissolve 4 teaspoons of meringue powder in 4 tablespoons of water.

4. Hold flower petals with tweezers. Apply thin, even layer of meringue mixture with paint brush. Any places not coated will turn brown.

5. With tweezers, hold petal over bowl and sprinkle with superfine sugar. Tap the tweezers to remove excess sugar, and repeat on other side.

6. Place on superfine sugar-coated wax paper to dry. Let dry in a cool place for 2-4 hours, longer if humidity is high.

7. When dry, pick up petals with tweezers and set into frosting. Sugared flowers can be made in advance and stored in an airtight container (for up to a year) in a cool dry place.

60

61

On a Sunday in August...

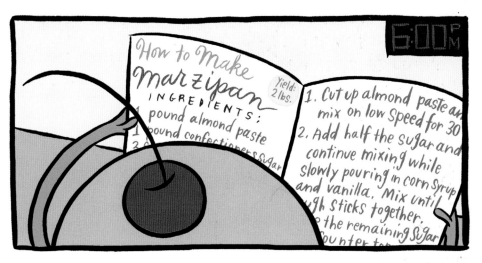

How to Make **marzipan**

Yield: 2 lbs.

INGREDIENTS:
1 pound almond paste
1 pound confectioners sugar

1. Cut up almond paste an mix on low speed for 30
2. Add half the sugar and continue mixing while slowly pouring in corn Syrup and vanilla. Mix until gh sticks together. e the remaining Sugar unter to

6:00 PM

ingredients

completed marzipan, rolled into ball

gel food colors

ALMOND PASTE

POWDERED SUGAR
10x   pure cane sugar

vanilla

Karo

TOOTH PICKS ROUND ROUND

petal dust (powdered food color)

x-acto knife

paintbrush

bowl of water

(kneading gel food color into smaller blobs of marzipan:)

Squish!   press!   squeeze!

Roll marzipan into small spheres and hemispheres.

Brush with water where shapes will attach.

Attach head to body.

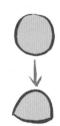

Roll out flat pieces of marzipan and cut shapes for ears and noses.

Brush with water where shapes will attach.

Attach shapes to head.

push!

Roll out flat pieces of marzipan and cut long rectangle for collar.

Brush with water on one side.

Attach around neck.

Paint on eyes with white gel food color and then use toothpick dipped in black gel color to make pupils.

Use toothpick dipped in red gel color (or color of your choice) to make freckles.

poke!

marzipan dog!

Use brush or toothpick and black gel food color to paint mouth.

Use brush and pink or red petal dust to put blush on cheeks...

marzipan cat!

(guard)

(Pet owners lined up to get into Church service to have their pets blessed.)

cat in carrier

hamster in clear ball

(Procession of the Animals, exiting after church service)

(wallaby)

a Few weeks later...

and a few months later. . .

(kneading dough)

(rolling out flat)

(pressing with cookie cutter)

ready for oven!

(portable table)

(biscuits)

sniff!

(Great Dane)

(Chihuahua)

Finally...

Valentine's Day...

chapter 4

101

CHAPTER 5

Bye, Eggplant. Have a great trip.

chapter 6

I can't wait to hear about your trip.

I hope you won't mind — I only have baking magazines.

138

Cupcake's

Repertoire

Raspberry Squares (From page 8)

ingredients:

Crust:
2 sticks unsalted
   butter, melted
2 cups all-purpose Flour

Filling:
1 cup raspberry
   preserves

topping:
2 1/4 cups all-purpose
   Flour
1 1/2 cups unpacked
   light brown sugar
2 sticks unsalted butter
   at room temperature,
   cut into smallish pieces

↑
9 by 13 inch glass
baking dish

1. Preheat oven to 350° F

2. For the crust, combine butter and Flour in a large bowl, until it becomes doughy.

3. Spread dough evenly into a 9 by 13 inch glass baking dish. You can use a large piece of waxed paper to press down the crust so it is Flat and even.

4. Bake the crust For 17 minutes. Let it cool completely beFore covering it with the Filling. As the crust cools, you can prepare the topping.

5. In a large bowl, mix the flour and the brown sugar.

6. Cut the butter into the flour and sugar with a pastry blender (or a fork,) until the mixture has the texture of coarse crumbs. Don't overmix it!

pastry blender

7. Once the crust is cool, spread the raspberry preserves evenly over the crust, leaving a 1/4 inch edge all around. (Any of the preserves that are touching the side of the pan will dry out when baking.)

8. Pour the topping evenly over the preserves.

9. Bake for 20-25 minutes until lightly browned.

10. Allow to cool before cutting into squares.

Brownies! (From page 52)

ingredients:

- 1 1/2 cups all-purpose flour
- 1 2/3 cups white sugar
- 1 teaspoon salt
- 6 large eggs, lightly beaten
- 1 teaspoon vanilla extract
- 1 2/3 cups (3 3/8 sticks) butter at room temperature
- 13 ounces high-quality bittersweet chocolate

Tip: You can save the paper wrappers from your butter to grease the pan— there should be just enough left over on them.

wipe!

1. Preheat oven to 350° F and grease a 9 by 13 inch glass pan with butter.

2. In a double boiler, small pan, or microwave, melt the chocolate and butter.

3. Whisk melted chocolate and butter until well blended and let cool.

4. While chocolate and butter mixture is cooling, whisk together eggs, sugar, and vanilla. They should become frothy and slightly lighter in color.

5. Carefully fold the cooled chocolate and butter mixture into the eggs. Whisk until everything is well mixed.

6. Fold in flour and salt. Mix thoroughly.

Lick!

Lick!

SUGAR
NT WT 2 LBS

7. Pour mixture into pan. Bake 32-37 minutes. Note: when they are done, the center of the brownies should still be a little gooey when you remove them from the oven.

8. Slice when cool.

Vanilla Cupcakes with Vanilla Frosting (From page 62)

The Cupcakes

ingredients:

2 sticks unsalted butter at room temperature

2 cups white sugar

4 large eggs at room temperature

1 1/2 cups self-rising flour

1 1/4 cups all-purpose flour

1 cup milk

1 teaspoon vanilla extract

1. Preheat oven to 350° F.

2. Line two 12-cup muffin tins or one 24-cup muffin tin with muffin papers. (If you make mini-cupcakes, this recipe will make 96! So you may want to cut the recipe in half for 48 mini-cupcakes. Also reduce the baking time by 1/3.)

3. In a large bowl, cream the butter until smooth, using an electric mixer on medium speed.

4. Add sugar gradually and beat until fluffy, around 3 minutes.

5. Add eggs one by one, beating well after adding each egg.

6. Combine flours in a bowl and whisk together.

7. Add flour mixture in three parts, alternating with milk and vanilla, and beating well (still using your electric mixer) after each addition.

8. Spoon the batter into the muffin papers so they are about 3/4 full.

9. Bake 20-22 minutes, until tops spring back when lightly touched.

10. Remove cupcakes from pan and cool completely before frosting.

the Frosting

ingredients:

2 sticks unsalted butter at room temperature
8 cups powdered sugar
1/2 cup milk
2 teaspoons vanilla extract

1. Place butter in a large mixing bowl.

2. Add 4 cups of sugar and all the milk and vanilla.

3. Beat like crazy with electric mixer, until smooth and creamy. (Note: Although you should mix on medium to high speed, start on the slowest setting or the powdered sugar will fly everywhere.)

4. Gradually add remaining sugar, 1 cup at a time, until frosting is the desired consistency. You most likely will not use all the sugar.

5. Store in a covered container at room temperature for up to three days.

to color your frosting, add a few drops of food coloring and mix thoroughly. Gel food colors work very nicely and come in a large selection of colors. You can find them at a baking supply shop or online. Use them sparingly – just a drop at a time – as they are very concentrated.

to frost regular-sized cupcakes, use a small rubber spatula, an offset spatula, or a butter knife. For mini-cupcakes, you can use a small spatula or piping tips.

Tools

Tips on using Piping Tips

21

12

(coupler)

6

30

You can use a pastry bag or a Ziploc bag fitted with a metal piping tip. (If using a Ziploc, snip off one corner and, from inside the bag, place the tip into the opening.) Using a rubber spatula, fill the bag with frosting. Starting at the outer edge, carefully pipe a circle around the cupcake, coiling it until you reach the center. Once you reach the center, stop squeezing the bag and pull upwards.

marzipan (From page 75)

ingredients:

- 1 pound (16 ounces) almond paste
- 1 pound (16 ounces) powdered sugar
- 3 ounces (by volume, not weight) light corn syrup
- 1 teaspoon vanilla extract

Almond paste comes in a can...

and almond paste comes in a roll, like a sausage.

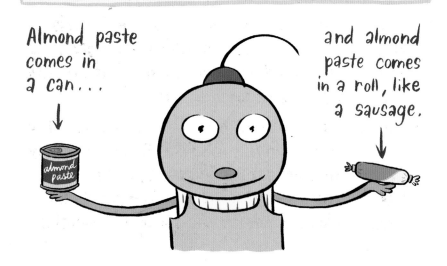

1. Cut up the almond paste into smallish pieces and place into bowl. Use electric mixer on low speed until oil begins to separate from the paste, about 30 seconds.

(IF you have a stand mixer like this, mix using the paddle attachment.)

2. Add half of the sugar and keep mixing while slowly pouring in corn syrup and vanilla. Continue to mix until the dough comes together and sticks to paddle or beaters. Unstick the dough.

3. Sift remaining sugar onto counter top.

4. Knead the sugar into the dough. If the dough is still sticky, you can knead in additional sugar. Keep kneading until the texture of the dough is fine and smooth. It should be soft but firm.

5. Thoroughly wrap the marzipan in plastic wrap. Then place in a sealed plastic bag, like a Ziploc, and store in refrigerator until ready to use. It can be kept in the refrigerator in a covered container for several weeks and kept in the freezer for up to 5 months.

Dog treats (From page 85)

Sniff!

Sniff!

Sniff!

Sniff!

ingredients:

- 1 egg
- 2 teaspoons dry yeast
- 1/2 cup lukewarm water
- 2 tablespoons dried parsley
- 1 1/2 cups chicken broth
- 3 tablespoons honey
- 5 cups whole wheat flour, more if necessary

1. Preheat oven to 350° F.

2. In a large bowl, combine yeast and warm water.

3. When the yeast has dissolved in the water, whisk in egg, parsley, broth, and honey.

4. Gradually blend in flour, until dough becomes stiff. You may need to add a little extra flour.

5. Transfer dough to a floured surface. Knead until smooth, about 3-5 minutes.

6. Shape dough into a ball, then use a rolling pin to roll to about 1/4 inch thick. Use a bone-shaped cookie cutter (or whatever shape you have handy) to cut out biscuits.

7. Transfer biscuits to ungreased baking sheets.

8. Consolidate scraps of dough, roll out again, and cut more biscuits.

9. Bake for 30 minutes. Remove from oven, flip biscuits over, and bake for 15 more minutes or until lightly browned on both sides.

10. Cool overnight and serve!

Peppermint Brownies (from page 90)

ingredients:

Brownies:
1 1/2 sticks unsalted butter
8 ounces bittersweet or semisweet chocolate
3 large eggs
1 1/2 cups sugar
3/4 cup all-purpose flour
1/2 teaspoon peppermint extract
1 teaspoon vanilla extract
1/4 teaspoon salt

Frosting:
2 cups sifted powdered sugar
1/2 stick unsalted butter at room temperature
2 tablespoons whole milk
3/4 teaspoon peppermint extract

1. Preheat oven to 350° F.

2. Grease a 9 by 13 inch glass baking pan.

3. Stir butter and chocolate in small saucepan over low heat until smooth. You can also melt them using a microwave. Set aside when melted.

4. Using electric mixer on medium speed, beat eggs and sugar in a large bowl until light and fluffy, about 5 minutes.

5. Add the chocolate and butter mixture, flour, salt, vanilla, and peppermint extract, and stir until just blended.

6. Pour batter into glass pan. Smooth out with a spoon or spatula. Bake for 25 minutes, or until a toothpick inserted into center comes out with moist crumbs attached. Cool before frosting.

7. For frosting, beat (using electric mixer) powdered sugar, butter, milk, and peppermint extract in bowl until creamy. You may need to add either more butter or powdered sugar to achieve desired texture. Also, you can add a little pink or green food color to make the frosting look mintier.

8. Spread frosting over brownies.

Special thanks to Melanie Schrimpe, who was kind enough to show me around her bakery "cheeks" in Williamsburg, Brooklyn; to let me take reference photos; and to explain the daily routine of running a bakeshop.

Extra big thanks also to Tanya McKinnon and, as always, my mom.

To my new friend miles: May your days be sweet.

cheeks Bakery, Brooklyn, 2005-2009